STICKER DRESSING ROMANS

Illustrated by Jean-Sébastien Deheeger
Designed by Emily Bornoff
Written by Louie Stowell

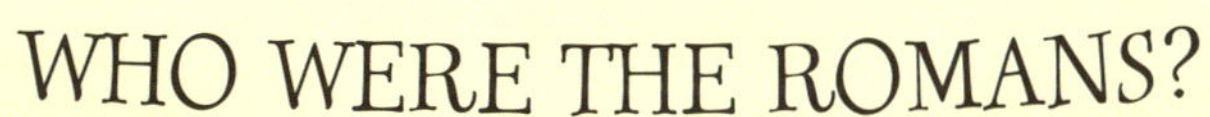

WHO WERE THE ROMANS?

Nearly 2,000 years ago, Rome, in Italy, was at the heart of a mighty empire, which stretched from the damp fields of England to the hot deserts of the Middle East. At the head of it all was a powerful Roman ruler called the Emperor.

CONTENTS

You'll find all the sticker pages in the middle of the book.

Historical consultant: Dr. Anne Millard

WELCOME TO ROME

Here at the port, you can see people from all over the Roman Empire. Romans often wear a sheet-like piece of wool, known as a toga, draped over a wool or linen tunic. The two Romans here are inspecting the goods of a trader from faraway Tyre, in the Middle East. The trader wears a sun hat and an embroidered tunic.

Wealthy Roman customer

Roman official

Trader from Tyre

AT THE FORUM

This is the main town square, or forum, in Rome. A priest, with his toga draped over his head, is on his way to sacrifice a bull to the Roman gods. Two foreign visitors, from Gaul (the Roman name for France) and Ethiopia, are dressed in their native costumes. The Ethiopian prince has just had his purse stolen, so he's not enjoying his visit.

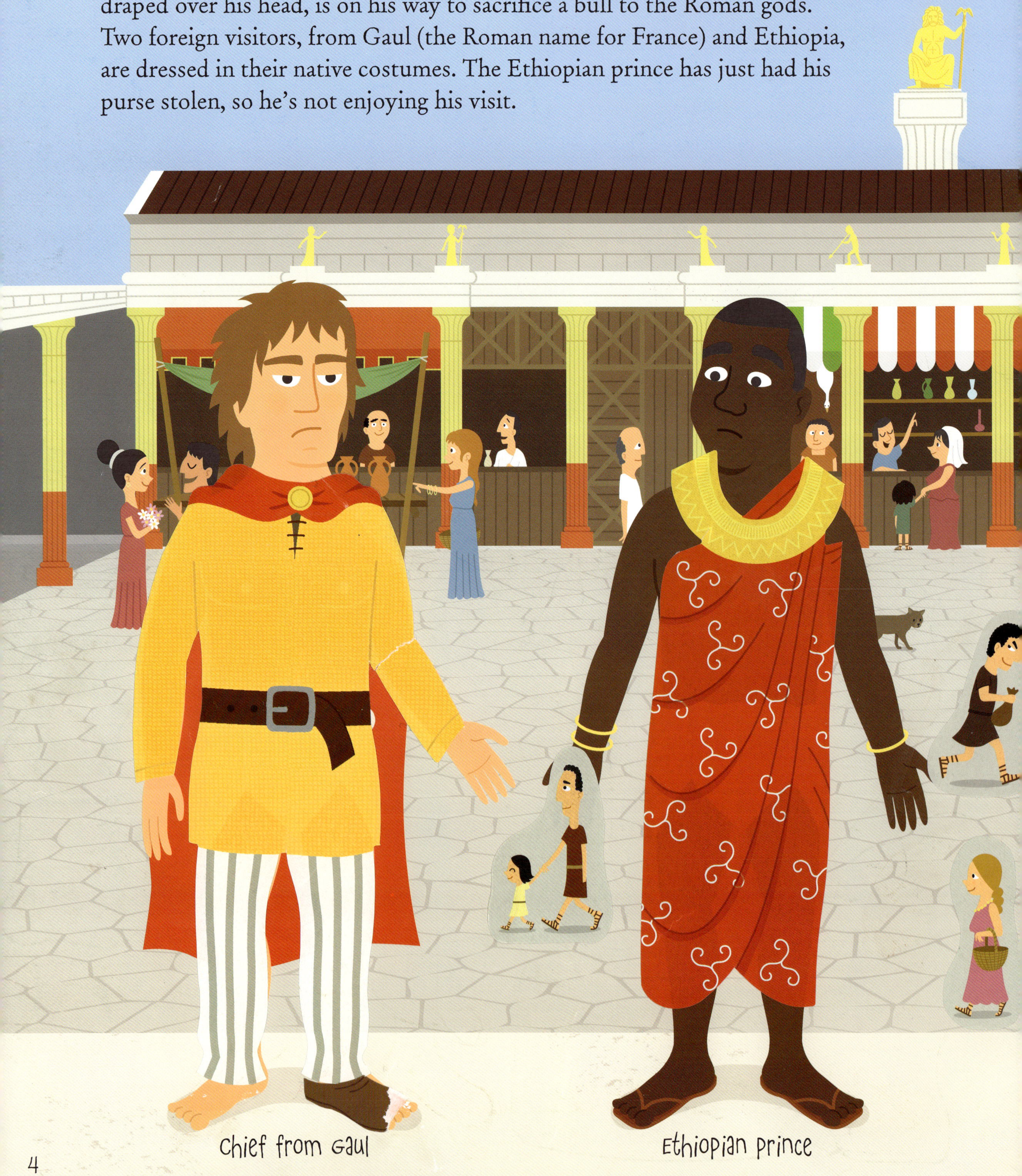

Chief from Gaul

Ethiopian prince

Roman priest

MASKED PLAYERS

In Roman plays, the actors wear masks to show what type of character they're playing. All the actors are men, even the one playing a girl. He wears a mask showing a girl's face, and cork high heels. All the masks are larger-than-life so people at the back of the audience can see them.

Actor playing a girl

Actor playing an old man

Actor playing a clown

SLAVES FOR SALE

Here at the slave market, slaves are sold as servants or to do dangerous jobs. The wealthy slave trader wears heavy gold chains over his tunic. The slaves don't wear much, so buyers can see they're fit and healthy. The slave from Britannia (Britain) has patterns on his skin, painted before he was captured.

Slave from Dacia in Eastern Europe

* This means he's really strong. It's in Latin, which is the language that the Romans speak.

Slave from Britannia

** This means he's a trained chariot driver.

IN THE CLASSROOM

These Roman schoolboys wear simple tunics and a pendant around their necks. Each pendant, called a bulla, is meant to give the boy who wears it magical protection. Their teacher is Greek and wears a loose costume that's similar to a Roman toga. He was once a slave but now he's a free man, after working for years as a private tutor to a rich Roman family.

Teacher

CHARIOT RACING

These chariot drivers wait nervously for their race to begin. Red, white, blue and green teams compete in every race, and each driver wears a tunic to match his team. Drivers wrap their horses' reins around their waists and carry a knife to cut themselves free if they fall.

Red team driver
Blue team driver

BATTLING GLADIATORS

Gladiators are slaves who fight to entertain big crowds. The 'Murmillo' and the 'Thracian' protect their arms with metal guards and wear helmets to shield their faces. All the gladiators wear leg guards and the 'Retiarius' carries a trident (a fork-shaped weapon) and a net.

Retiarius gladiator

Thracian gladiator
Murmillo gladiator

IN THE SENATE

The Emperor is giving a speech in a building known as the Senate, where Roman politicians meet. He's dressed in a purple toga – only emperors may wear these – and a crown of gold leaves. The consul (his right-hand man) has a toga with a purple stripe. The Emperor's bodyguard is heavily armed at all times, in case someone tries to attack the Emperor.

Emperor's bodyguard

ARMY CAMP

A legionary (ordinary soldier) wears a helmet and a breastplate made from strips of metal. He's always getting shouted at by the centurion (his superior officer), who wears a feathered helmet. The legate (the officer in charge of the whole camp) wears a shiny breastplate, a skirt of leather strips, a fancy helmet, leather boots, and a cloak.

Legionary (ordinary soldier)

Centurion (commander)
Legate (the boss)

A VICTORY PARADE

The Roman army has won a big battle and they're celebrating with a parade. The barbarian chief they were fighting wears a striped tunic. (Romans called most people from outside the Empire barbarians.) The standard bearer, known as the Aquilifer, carries the eagle symbol that stands for Rome, and wears a lion's skin on his head.

Barbarian Chief

Aquilifer
General

ROMAN FEAST

It's party time at the house of a wealthy Roman. The host is dressed in a special party toga known as a synthesis and he's reading out one of his own poems. The musician wears an orange tunic to match the other male entertainers and carries an aulus (a type of flute). The host's slaves all wear blue tunics.

CARMEN

Musician

Host

Server

A SYRIAN PRINCE

On the eastern side of the Roman Empire is a land called Syria. A Syrian prince is having a meeting with some Roman soldiers who are helping him fight off bandits. He wears fancy robes and lots of jewels.

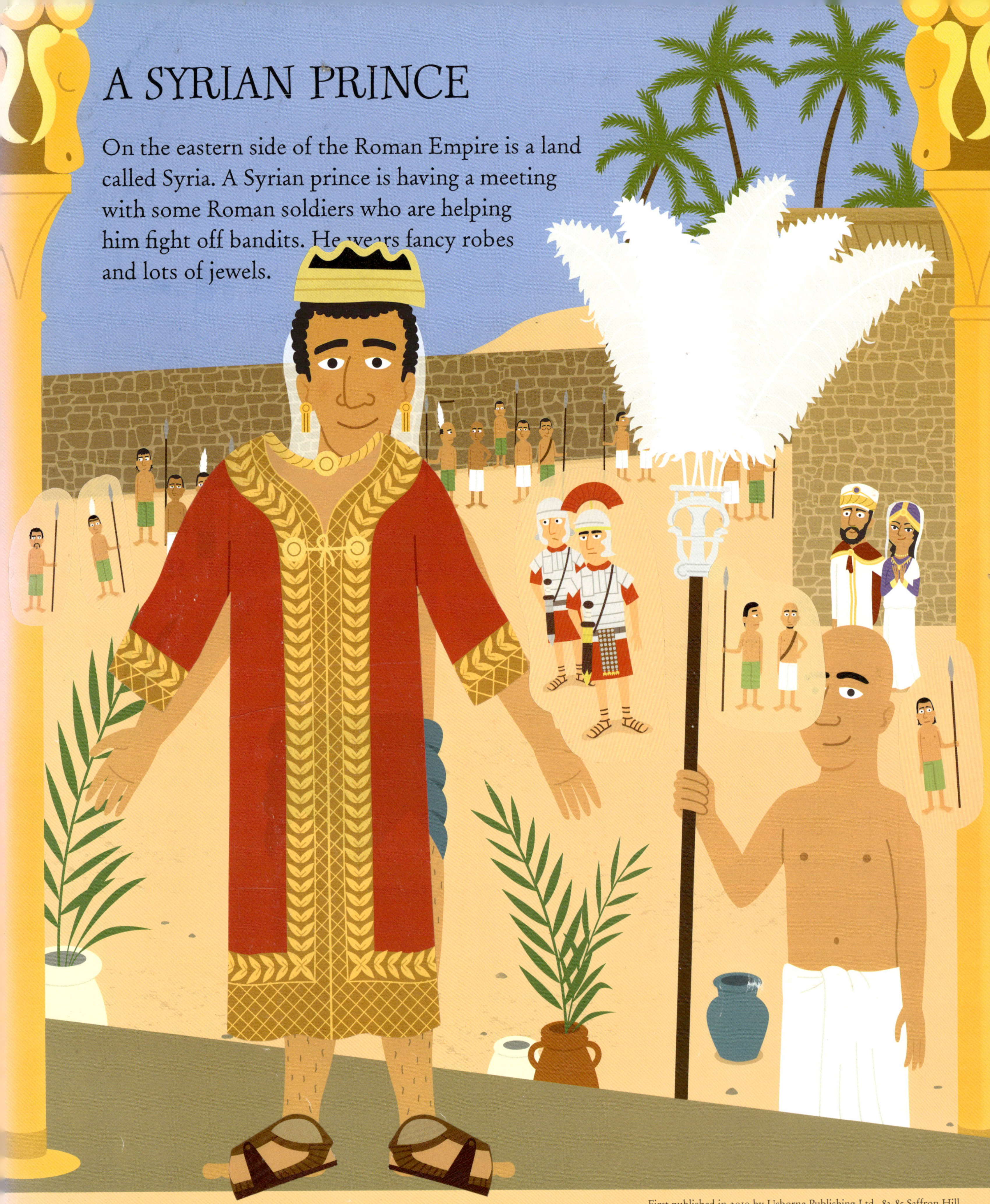

A prince of Syria

First published in 2010 by Usborne Publishing Ltd., 83-85 Saffron Hill, London, EC1N 8RT, England. www.usborne.com. First published in America in 2011. UE.